Come Sit By Me

Dedicated to all the children who have or will have HIV / AIDS.

The name Nicholas means victory for the people.

Canadian Cataloguing Information

Merrifield, Margaret.
Come sit by me

ISBN 0-88961-141-6

1. AIDS (Disease) in children - Juvenile fiction.
I. Collins, Heather. II. Title.

PS8576.E77C6 1990   jC813'.54   C90-094610-5
PZ7.M47Co 1990

Published by Women's Press
517 College Street, Suite 233
Toronto, Ontario, Canada M6G 4A2

This book was produced by the collective effort
of Women's Press and was a project of the
Young Readers Manuscript Group.

Women's Press gratefully acknowledges financial
support from the Canada Council, the Ontario
Arts Council, the Toronto Board of Health and
the AIDS Committee of London, Ontario.

Printed and bound in Canada by union labour.

Come Sit by Me

by Margaret Merrifield M.D.   Illustrated by Heather Collins

An educational storybook about AIDS and HIV infection
for small children ages 4 to 8 and their caregivers.

women's
P R E S S

Karen woke up bright and early. She tiptoed into the big bedroom, snuggled into bed and whispered to her mother, "Is it a school day or a stay-home day?"

"A school day," answered Mother sleepily.

"Hmmph." Karen crossed her arms and pouted. "I like stay-home days better."

Summer holidays were over.

What fun they had had swimming ...collecting treasures ...rolling down sand dunes ...staying up late ...visiting Grandpa and Grandma.

"But I want to stay home with you!" she said to Father.

Father answered in the gentlest of ways, "Now Karen, go and get ready. You'll be happy to see your friends and maybe there will be new friends to play with."

So Mother went to her work. Father went to his work. Her older brother Michael went to his big school and Karen got to go to hers.

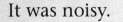

It was noisy.

When Benjamin saw Karen he yelled, "Karen, Karen, come sit by me!"

Erica yelled even louder, "Karen, come sit by me!"

Everyone giggled, and wiggled on their bottoms to make room for Karen in the snack-time circle.

"It's so nice to have you back Karen. We missed you. Would you like to be the special helper today?" asked Julie her teacher.

"Yes, please!" Her smile got bigger and bigger as she helped serve crackers and juice to her friends.

She was happy almost all of the day climbing, swinging, painting and playing pretend.

That day they played doctor.

"My mother's a doctor, so I get to be the doctor," Karen said.

"I'll be the sick person," Erica said.

"I'll be the nurse," added Benjamin.

Together they rescued Erica from a burning house, made wet paper casts for her broken legs and gave medicine for Jonathan's fever.

They all got better.

Nicholas was the new
child in their group.
　He was quiet.
　He wasn't rude.
　He didn't play much.
　He minded his manners at
lunch.

That night Karen told
Mother about her day.
"I had fun playing. I had a
really good nap. I didn't
have to take a time out.
Nicholas isn't my
friend yet."

The days got colder and colder. Everyone had to wear long pants. One day Karen told her family that Nicholas was sick and that she missed him.

"He's my best friend now," she said sadly.

"How many days has he been sick?" Mother asked.

"I don't know. A lot," she answered.

After many sleeps, Nicholas was feeling better and came back to school.

"What's AIDS?" Karen asked one night at supper.

"AIDS is a sickness. Why do you ask?" asked Father.

"Because Sebastian said he can't play with Nicholas anymore because Nicholas has AIDS."

"Do you play with Nicholas?" Michael asked.

"Yes, he's my friend," she answered.

"Does he look sick?" her brother asked.

"I don't know." Karen shrugged her answer and continued to eat her spaghetti.

Mother sat down close to Karen and told her this...

"When you get sick with a fever, a cough or a runny nose, thousands of healthy fighter cells in your blood help make you get better.

"But if Nicholas has AIDS, some of the most important fighter cells in his blood can't fight anymore. They can't help him get better from his fever, cough or runny nose like yours do."

Karen asked, "If I play with him, will I get AIDS?"

"No," answered Mother. "You can play with Nicholas, eat with him, sleep by him, hug him, and do the things you normally do with all the other children."

So she did. She was happy. She had no
worries.

But some of the parents wouldn't let their
children play with Karen because she
played with Nicholas.

When Mother and Father
found this out, they were
extremely upset. They called
all the parents. They called
all the teachers and said,
"We need to have a
meeting and talk about
AIDS."

Everyone came.
They talked and talked
late into the night and
they all learned a lot
about HIV and AIDS.

You CANNOT get
AIDS OR HIV By...

The next day, the children started to talk about dinosaurs.

They hunted for dinosaur bones in the sandbox and planned to make dinosaur soup for lunch. At circle time, they marched and sang:

"I am a Brontosaurus
I'm a stocky stompin' dinosaur
up on my back are many many children
with lots of room for more"

Nicholas was the last to arrive.

When he saw what they were playing he shouted, "I know a lot about dinosaurs! You don't have to be afraid of them."

Sebastian yelled, "Nicholas, come sit by me!"

Benjamin yelled even louder, "Nicholas, come sit by me!"

But Karen yelled the loudest of all, "No, Nicholas, come sit by me!!"

Everyone giggled, and wiggled on their bottoms to make room for Nicholas in the snack-time circle.

"Nicholas, would you like to be the special helper today?" asked Julie.

"Yes please," said Nicholas.

And he was.

Many People are worried about getting HIV or AIDS.* Mo

Living with someone who has HIV or AIDS

Sitting next to someone

Caring for animals

Sharing a toilet or bathroom

Sharing cups and plates, knives and forks

Having your hair cut

Mosquito bites

Shaking or holding hands

orries are unnecessary. You **cannot** get HIV or AIDS by:

Taking a nap
next to someone

Touching clothes
or used tissues

Hugging
someone

From coughs, sneezes
or talking to someone

Sharing toys

Swimming in
a pool or lake

Playing with
someone

Eating and
drinking

*AIDS is short for Acquired Immune Deficiency Syndrome. HIV is short for Human Immunodeficiency Virus.

Information for Students, Parents, Teachers and Caregivers About HIV and AIDS

Introduction

AIDS/HIV is as much a social problem as it is a medical one.

AIDS is a broad topic which touches on other challenging moral and personal issues such as sexuality, sickness, death, and acceptance. Many people want to believe the AIDS problem will just go away. It will not. AIDS is now everyone's concern because millions of people world-wide are silently infected with HIV (see below) and don't know it. This section is written to help *you*, as educators and caregivers, to understand AIDS so that you can provide children with some practical answers to the many questions about this disease. Children model parents' and teachers' behaviour. That is why you must put aside your fears or indifference and learn about AIDS. If you can answer your children's questions about AIDS in a direct and honest way while they are young, they may discover you as a good source of information later on as well.

Many things about AIDS are still uncertain, such as the number of people infected and how to treat it. **What is certain is the knowledge of how you can protect yourself from AIDS.**

Quarantine is only applied to infectious diseases which are spread by ordinary daily activities. AIDS is *not* spread this way.

What is AIDS?

AIDS is the shortened name for **A**cquired **I**mmune **D**eficiency **S**yndrome. AIDS was first identified in the early 1980s. AIDS is caused by a very unusual **virus** called **HIV**. HIV weakens the human defence or **immune** system so the body is unable to protect itself from infections and cancers.

Strictly speaking, "AIDS" refers only to the last stages of HIV infection when a person becomes very sick. There are several stages of HIV infection. The first stage has no symptoms or mild symptoms, which usually clear up.

What is an immune system?

Think of your immune system as your personal health army.

Everyone's body is made up of the same parts. For example, your muscles and bones make up one system so that you can walk and move. The body's health protection system is called the **immune system**. Its job is to identify and fight off anything harmful that has gotten into the body. This defence system has millions of "fighters" called "white cells." They live in the blood, always ready to attack invaders. If a germ or virus gets into the body, it meets this inner defence system. That's why you get better from a cold or the chicken pox. When you get a fever, that's one way of knowing that a fight is going on inside your body.

What is a virus?

There are many different germs that cause diseases. Thousands lie on our skin or float in the air we breathe. Some of these germs are helpful to us. Some can harm us. The very smallest germs are called **viruses**. Viruses are so small that millions can fit on the tip of a pencil. Viruses cause common diseases such as colds, flu, measles, and chicken pox.

What exactly is HIV?

HIV is the name of the virus that is associated with the sickness "AIDS."

HIV is the shortened name for **H**uman **I**mmunodeficiency **V**irus. If you think of HIV infection as a 1-to-15 year process, you can understand why it is such a problem in the world, both culturally and physically. **The majority of people who are infected with HIV do not develop *any* symptoms of the sickness called AIDS for a long time, but they can still pass the virus to others.**

Person gets infected with HIV	**1 to 15 years later**	**AIDS**
HIV is passed from an infected person to an uninfected person through blood, semen, or vaginal secretions.	The person begins to feel unwell; e.g. night sweats with unexplained weight loss. Some people call this phase ARC (AIDS-Related Complex).	The person gets *very* sick from unusual infections and cancers that uninfected people don't get.

How does HIV damage the body's defence system?

HIV is a very unusual virus. The defence system has special fighter cells that work like alarm clocks to wake up the army when an invader attacks. HIV specifically attacks these alarm clock cells one by one so that they can't work properly any more. Over time (years) HIV eventually turns off all the alarm clock cells, and the rest of the army doesn't realize there are invaders present. Once this happens, people with HIV get very sick, and most die.

How does HIV get into the body?

It's not who you are but what you do that gets you infected with HIV.

The only way to get HIV infection is to have *direct* exchange of blood, semen, or vaginal secretions from an HIV-infected person. **There are only four ways to do this.**

1. Having **sexual intercourse with an infected person**. Now, more than ever, it is vital that we talk about sex and sexuality openly and honestly. Because most people do not even know that they have HIV in their bodies, you have to be smart to be safe when it comes to HIV, AIDS, and sexual intercourse. How? Use latex condoms correctly.

2. Drug users who **share needles** for steroid injections, tattoos, or street drugs can unknowingly pass HIV to each other. This can be prevented by cleaning the needles with household bleach. If you donate blood or get a shot, doctors and other medical people always use fresh, clean needles. You can ask to make sure.

3. Many **babies born to HIV-infected mothers** are infected.

4. Some people became infected with HIV from blood transfusions and medicines made from blood between 1978 and 1985. Since 1985, developed countries have been testing blood for HIV.

How can I know if I have HIV in my body?

Most people who have HIV look and feel healthy for years. When the immune system first identifies HIV it makes **antibodies**. These antibodies can be found through a simple **blood test**. A positive test means that you were infected with HIV and could now infect someone else.

Is there a medicine to get HIV out of the body?

No. Doctors and researchers are working hard to treat the unusual diseases of AIDS, and to develop vaccines and medicines that can repair damaged alarm-clock fighter cells and stop HIV from damaging the immune system.

Can I get HIV from mosquitoes or animals?

No. HIV cannot live in the bodies of mosquitoes or animals, so it is not spread by insects or pets.

Can I get AIDS from kissing?

Thousands of AIDS cases have been reported world-wide. No cases reported have been caused by kissing. Very small traces of AIDS virus have been found in saliva, but it is **blood and semen** that you have to worry about, not saliva.

How can I protect myself from HIV?

1. HIV infection is a sexually transmitted disease. Practice **safer sex**. If you have sexual intercourse with someone who has had past partners, or if you have had past partners, and both of you have not had a recent negative HIV blood test, then it is wise for the man *always* to use latex **condoms**. Women should insist

that their partners use condoms. Women should use **spermicidal foam** so that if the condom breaks the foam will help kill any virus. Condoms with foam also provide protection against other sexually transmitted diseases and pregnancy.

2. Learn the many ways of **expressing affection** besides intercourse.

3. **Never share needles** for any reason whatsoever. If you have sexual intercourse with anyone who has shared or is sharing needles, always use latex condoms and foam.

4. **There has been no evidence that HIV is transmitted through minor cuts in daycare or school situations.** HIV is a fragile virus and dies very quickly outside the body. If any child has a cut, cover it, and clean up any blood with a **dilute bleach solution** (nine parts water to one part bleach).

Summary

HIV infection is much easier to prevent than to treat. Learn about HIV and AIDS so you can be safe.

- There is *no* evidence to suggest that HIV is spread by casual daily activities.
- If you participate in one of these three activities you may become infected:
    1. Being born to an HIV-infected mother.
    2. Having sexual intercourse with an HIV-infected partner.
    3. Sharing needles with someone who is infected with HIV.
- Remember, most people infected with HIV don't know they are.
- Children or adults with damaged immune systems from HIV can easily become ill from diseases that people with healthy immune systems may give them (e.g., colds). Good hygiene is important in all caregiving places, for everyone.

What should I tell children?

1. **AIDS is a serious sickness but it is very hard for a child to get.**

2. Review and discuss the picture page on the ways you *can't* get HIV/AIDS.

3. If you have small children, be aware that they perceive your own attitudes about sexuality and relationships from a very early age. Be open to questions. If they ask, tell them the truth about how you *can* get HIV/AIDS, but in simple terms:

    e.g., "People get HIV/AIDS in two ways — from getting blood from an HIV/AIDS person into their own body or by having sexual intercourse with someone who is infected." You can explain what sexual intercourse is and that it is for grownups, not children.

4. Review the **bolded** sections with older children. As your own understanding about HIV infection grows, you should be able to answer their questions.

    e.g., "Condoms are like thin balloons that men wear over their 'privates' or penis during sex to stop the spread of germs."

    e.g., "If you find needles, don't touch them; and never use drugs that aren't given for a medical reason, especially needle drugs."

Resources

1. Physicians. Local Public Health Units. AIDS Hotlines/Committees: (The 800 numbers are toll free.)
   Canada:
   BC 1-800-972-2437;
   Alta 1-800-772-2437;
   Sask 1-800-667-7766;
   Man 1-800-782-2437;
   Ont 1-800-668-2437;
   Qué 1-800-463-5656;
   NB 1-800-561-4009;
   NS and PEI 1-(902)-425-2437;
   Nfld 1-(709)-579-8656;
   NWT 1-(403)-920-6542;
   YT 1-(403)-668-6461;
   U.S.A. 1-800-342-2437.

2. *Does AIDS Hurt: Educating young children (ages 1-12) about AIDS*, by Marcia Quackenbush, M.S., and Sylvia Villarreal, M.D. (1988) Network Publications, Santa Cruz, California 95061-1830. ISBN 0-941816-52-4. $20.00 U.S. This book for adults has examples of questions and answers for each age group. Ask your library to order a copy.

3. *Safe, Smart Sex, Especially for Teenagers*, by Liz Braun (1987). 316 Indian Road, Toronto, Ontario, Canada, M3H 5T5. ISBN 0-921014-05-8. $5.95.. This witty and practical easy read book is for anyone 13 and over. This is the book to give your teenager.